GW00863390

Terr

Tuesday

Written by

Felicity Field

Illustrated by Ray Shuell

This story is dedicated to my lovely niece, Emily, who despite her problems with English, went on to enjoy a highly successful career in Marketing. Her problems didn't suddenly disappear but her engaging personality and sheer determination to succeed, shone through. When asked the secret of her success, Emily replied:

"I'm fearless, I'm resilient and I can talk to anyone."

Tuesday again – 'Terrible Tuesday' Daisy called it. Just the thought of English all day with Mrs Thistle was enough to make her feel queasy.

Daisy found English very tricky indeed. If it hadn't been for story time in the afternoon, Tuesday would have been utterly unbearable. But as much as she hated grammar and spelling, she loved to listen to stories and liked to make up her own. Her best friend, Lily, said she had a talent for storytelling and a great imagination. Writing was a different matter though, and a real problem for Daisy. However hard she tried, she still managed to get her letters back to front and upside down, every which way but the right way. It was all very upsetting.

"I can't do it, I just can't," she would protest.

On one occasion her frustration really got the better of her and she hurled her workbook across the classroom, narrowly missing the top of Mrs Thistle's head. Some would have said that was a pity and nearly impossible, since Mrs Thistle's hair stretched almost to the ceiling.

At school Daisy's achievements were few. She had never won the class prize for English, or any other subject for that matter. Not like Dan - 'Hand in the air, please Miss,' Dan, always ready to thank Mrs Thistle for *this* and help her out with *that*. So creepy, he once wrote a poem entitled "World's Best Teacher" and dedicated it to Mrs Thistle. She, of course, found it "Simply excellent," and "Beautifully written." *Well, she would, wouldn't she?* thought Daisy.

But there were no such encouraging words for Daisy. "Must try harder," Mrs Thistle would say in a manner as prickly as her hairstyle. Daisy tried to hide her embarrassment. She would shrug her shoulders and giggle as if she didn't care. But Daisy did care. She cared a great deal. Even Lily didn't know how much she really cared. She cared so much that when she got home she would lock herself in her bedroom and sob into her pillow, and when she couldn't sob another sob, she would turn to Kitt.

Kitt looked much older than his seven years. He was a good listener and was always there for Daisy. She sometimes spent hours talking to him. With Kitt she shared everything – her happy times and her worries too. He offered no response but his kind, worn face and shiny bright eyes were a comfort to her. A photograph of them together on her second birthday had pride of place on her bedroom wall. It reminded her how handsome he was then. His fur was thick and fluffy and the brown velvet pads on his paws had felt soft against her skin. For a Teddy Bear he had particularly large ears and a cute turned up nose, embroidered in black thread. But time had not been kind to Kitt. His once-dense coat had become sparse and grubby. Thick, cotton stuffing peeped out from his paws where his pads were torn and frayed, and his ears had been sewn back so many times they were half the size they used to be. The circumstances surrounding the loss of his arm were still unclear. Something to do with next-door's Labrador, Daisy suspected. All she knew for sure was that it was found, buried with a large bone, in the flowerbed at the end of the garden. But Kitt's ragged looks didn't matter to Daisy – she loved him, just because she did.

"Terrible Tuesday again," Daisy complained to Lily as they walked arm in arm to school.

"Don't worry, Daisy, it'll be over before you know it and we can go to the park later."

"She's going to pick on me, Lily, she always does."

"Daisy," Lily said thoughtfully, "are you going to enter a story for the Year 4 English Competition?"

"Don't be silly, Lily. With Thistle Head as a judge and my problems with English, I don't think so. Why? Are you?"

"No, Maths is my best subject but your stories are good, Daisy, you should enter."

Daisy hadn't been entirely truthful. She did want to enter a story and thought the one she handed in the

Tuesday before was her best ever. If Mrs Thistle was even a tiny bit encouraging about it, she would enter it for the English Competition. She hadn't told Lily because she didn't want to raise anyone's hopes, especially her own. Secretly she thought it had a real chance, particularly since she'd taken so much care with grammar and spelling. Surely even Mrs Thistle would see the potential in it.

When story time came Daisy's heart pounded like a drum. She felt a mixture of excitement and terror as she waited for the stories to be returned. After singling out the usual students for praise, Mrs Thistle said, "One student has produced a particularly outstanding piece of work this week."

Daisy went weak at the knees. She closed her eyes and wished for her name to be called.

"Congratulations, Dan, it's an excellent story. You should consider entering it for the Year 4 English Competition."

Daisy's eyes welled heavy with tears and when her story was returned with bright red splodges marking each mistake, she felt quite hopeless. "You really must try harder. Your work is full of errors," said Mrs Thistle, "and next time, do try and write something that's not quite so ridiculous."

Daisy breathed a sigh of relief when the bell rang at the end of the day. She quickly shoved her story into her school bag and ran towards home with tears streaming down her face. Lily only just managed to catch up with her. "Hang on, Daisy, aren't we going to the park?" she shouted.

"No, Mum said I had to be home early, sorry," Daisy replied, fighting back the tears.

"Are you okay?" asked Lily, concerned.

"Yes, Lily, I'm fine; you go on now. I'll see you tomorrow."

When Daisy got home she managed to avoid everyone, dashed upstairs and locked herself in her room.

"Daisy, is everything all right?" her mum shouted from downstairs.

"Yes, Mum," she replied trying to disguise her teary voice. "I just want to get my homework done. I'll be down soon."

With that, she flopped onto her bed, buried her head in her pillow to muffle the sound, and cried and cried.

After a while she turned to Kitt. "Oh Kitt, I'm so unhappy," she sobbed, rocking backwards and forwards as she clutched him to her cheek. "Why can't I do anything right? I spent so long on that story. It was such a special story and old Thistle Head said it was ridiculous. Well it is ridiculous, isn't it?"

She screwed up the story and threw it into the bin by her bed.

"Of course Dan's story was excellent. His stories always are. Thistle Head said so and Thistle Head is always right. Oh Kitt, if only I could talk to you properly. How I wish you could speak."

"But I can speak, Daisy."

Daisy almost fell off the bed in shock.

"Kitt, is that really you talking?"

"Oh yes, Daisy, it's me," replied Kitt, in a deep, soft voice.

"Kitt, you can speak!"

"So it seems," said Kitt.

"But how? I mean why? I mean, I don't understand..."

"Neither do I really."

"But you've never spoken before, Kitt."

"You've never wished me to before. Now, about your story. Do you believe in it, Daisy?"

"Of course I do, especially now," she replied with great conviction.

"Then stick with it. Don't let Thistle Head, I mean Mrs Thistle, put you off. If you think it's a good story, have the courage to stick with it."

"It's no use, Kitt. Even if I did enter it for the English Competition, I'll never win with Thistle Head as a judge. Anyway, look at all these mistakes." She held up her workbook for him to see.

"You can sort that out, Daisy."

"It's not as easy as that. You know better than anyone
what a problem it is for me."

"How much do you want to win the English
Competition?" Kitt asked sternly.

"Silly question. It would mean everything to me."

"Then correct it. Sometimes the things we really want,
the things really worth having, don't come easily. Just think
how you'll feel if you win, it'll be worth the effort. Well?"

"Okay, okay," shouted Daisy throwing her arms in the air. "You win, Kitt, you win."

Daisy retrieved her story from the bin, took a dictionary from the bookshelf, switched on her desk lamp and set to work. She frowned and tutted, thumbed carefully from letter to letter in the dictionary, and considered every word and sentence with the utmost care. Impressed that she was working so hard, her mum brought up some dinner on a tray. Daisy was too busy to notice the hours flying by. Occasionally she glanced over at Kitt and caught him napping. Finally she jumped up from her chair.

"Hurrah, I've finished. Kitt, I've finished, Hurrah," she shouted.

By then Kitt was sound asleep. Quite satisfied with her efforts she sneaked into bed beside him, kissed him on the forehead and hugged him tightly till she drifted off too.

As she started to wake next morning, Daisy wondered if she had been dreaming. She turned to Kitt who was snoring loudly beside her. "It's true, Kitt, wake up, it's true, isn't it - you can speak?"

"Morning Daisy, sleep well?" Kitt asked as he yawned and stretched his one arm slowly above his head. "Now, Daisy," he said sleepily, "make sure you give your story to Thistle He… I mean Mrs Thistle, first thing."

"Don't worry, after all that effort I won't forget," she assured him.

At the first opportunity, Daisy handed Mrs Thistle her story.

"I'd like to enter this one for the Year 4 English Competition," she said.

"But this is the same, rather ridiculous story I returned to you yesterday, isn't it?" Mrs Thistle replied, eyebrows raised.

"That's right," said Daisy bravely. "I've corrected it and I'd like to enter it please."

"Very well," agreed Mrs Thistle puzzled, and reluctantly added Daisy's story to the list of entries.

The last day of term had arrived. Winners of the Year 4 prizes would be announced that morning and the butterflies in Daisy's tummy fluttered madly as she waited for Lily to call for her. On the way to school she finally told Lily that she had entered a story after all. Her best friend was delighted and understood the reasons why Daisy hadn't confided in her before.

"There's something else I want to tell you, Lily," Daisy said with an air of mystery, "but I'll leave that till later if you don't mind."

Lily asked no questions. "Okay, Daisy," she said cheerfully and they continued on their way.

The Assembly Hall was bursting at the seams. Daisy and Lily sat together fidgeting nervously as they waited for the winners to be announced. A panel of judges was lined up on stage but Mrs Thistle was missing. As soon as the Head Mistress stood up to speak the Hall fell silent.

"Welcome to our prize-giving ceremony," she said. "Before we announce the winners, I am sorry to say that one of our judges cannot be with us today. Unfortunately when Mrs Thistle was leaving school last Tuesday her hair became tangled in a ceiling light and she suffered a shock. She will make a full recovery but it will take several months for her hair to grow back. In her absence, Miss Rose has joined the panel of judges and will also be covering her classes." Daisy and Lily erupted with delight and only just managed to conceal their giggles.

There was great excitement as the winners were announced. To her amazement Lily won the prize for Maths. Daisy clapped for her so hard her hands began to sting. Miss Rose was asked to present the English prize. She was young and pretty with soft, dainty features and a warm smile. Daisy liked her instantly.

"I am delighted to present the Year 4 prize for English," she said. "The standard was very high but after careful consideration I am pleased to announce that the prize goes to..."

Daisy clenched Lily's hand and wished for her name to be announced.

"Dan, congratulations your story was very well written."

Pretending not to care, Daisy shrugged her shoulders as she always did.

"Never mind," Lily whispered. "There's always next year."

With a smug smile the width of a banana Dan rose from his chair and slowly made his way towards the stage, keen to show off the shiny, new, black-patent shoes his mum had bought him just for the occasion. 'Winners Shoes,' she called them. He couldn't have known it, but Mr Poppy the school caretaker, well known for his fastidious nature, had been particularly particular in preparing the Hall that morning. He swept and polished, scrubbed and rubbed until everything sparkled like a new pin.

So shiny were the steps leading to the stage that when the sole of Dan's shiny, new, black-patent left shoe connected with the shiniest top step, he slipped so spectacularly that he was launched onto the stage like a rocket, landing squarely in the Head Mistress's lap - to her absolute horror! After some while the laughter in the Hall faded, and both Dan and the Head Mistress had recovered enough to continue with the prize-giving. Still a little winded, Dan proudly, but rather less smugly, received his award from Miss Rose.

Then, to everyone's surprise, Miss Rose continued: "This year we have decided to award two prizes for English. One story was truly inspiring. The story of Kitt, the talking teddy bear, was both charming and funny. This student has a vivid imagination and although the grammar was shaky at times, she demonstrates a real talent for storytelling. Daisy, well done indeed."

Daisy's nerves disappeared in a flash. She bounded onto the stage grinning from ear to ear and proudly accepted her prize from Miss Rose.

Bursting with joy, Daisy and Lily skipped home stopping only to admire their certificates and discuss which books they would buy with the tokens they were awarded.

"I told you your stories were good," said Lily.

"Thanks for believing in me, Lily. I'm glad I have a best friend like you. Remember I said there was something else I wanted to tell you? Well, my story, you know, about Kitt. It wasn't exactly a story. Well, it was when I wrote it but now it's not, if you see what I mean?"

"You're not making any sense, Daisy."

"Well, you know my teddy bear is called Kitt?"

"Yes?"

"Well he does talk, or at least he does now."

"How exciting," Lily said casually.

"You believe me then, Lily?"

"Of course I do," said Lily, like the true friend she was. "Will he talk to me?"

"I'll ask him, Lily, maybe tomorrow."

"Okay," said Lily, "see you tomorrow."

As soon as Daisy got home she ran upstairs to tell Kitt.

"I won the English prize Kitt, isn't it fantastic?" she squealed. "You said it would be worth the effort and it was."

Kitt didn't answer.

"Kitt, Kitt, isn't it great?"

Still Kitt said nothing. Daisy did everything she could to get Kitt to speak. She even tickled him under the arm to see if it would make him laugh but nothing seemed to work. Suddenly Daisy realised something. She took her story from her school bag, 'Kitt's Story,' she had called it, and read the verse that was its ending.

When words were not needed to help anymore
Kitt's voice disappeared, even his snore
But Kitt was still there as ever before
A silent dear friend with a frayed, funny paw

Now I understand, Daisy thought. She gently took Kitt's paw and danced him round the bedroom. "Thank you, Kitt," she said, "I'm just so happy. Tuesday will be terrific in future. 'Terrific Tuesday' I think I'll call it."

Printed in Great Britain
by Amazon